Hello, Family Members,

Learning to read is one of the most ir̲ ̲ ̲ ̲ ̲ ̲ ̲
of early childhood. **Hello Reader!** b̲ ̲ ̲ ̲ ̲
children become skilled readers who like to read. Beginning
readers learn to read by remembering frequently used words
like "the," "is," and "and"; by using phonics skills to decode new
words; and by interpreting picture and text clues. These books
provide both the stories children enjoy and the structure they
need to read fluently and independently. Here are suggestions
for helping your child.

- Have your child think about a word he or she does not
  recognize right away. Provide hints such as "Let's see if we
  know the sounds" and "Have we read other words like this
  one?"
- Encourage your child to use phonics skills to sound out new
  words.
- Provide the word for your child when more assistance is
  needed so that he or she does not struggle and the experi-
  ence of reading with you is a positive one.
- Encourage your child to have fun by reading with a lot of
  expression . . . like an actor!

I do hope that you and your child enjoy this book.

> —Francie Alexander
> Reading Specialist,
> Scholastic's Learning Ventures

Activity Pages

In the back of the book are skill-building activities. These are designed to
give children further reading and comprehension practice and to provide
added enjoyment. Offer help with directions as needed and encourage
your child to have FUN with each activity.

Game Cards

In the middle of the book are eight pairs of game cards. These are designed
to help your child become more familiar with words in the book and to
play fun games.
- Have your child use the word cards to find matching words in the story.
Then have him or her use the picture cards to find matching words in the
story.
- Play a matching game. Here's how: Place the cards face up. Have your
child match words to pictures. Once the child feels confident matching
words to pictures, put cards face down. Have the child lift one card, then
lift a second card to see if both match. If the cards match, the child can
keep them. If not, place the cards face down once again.
Keep going until he or she finds all matches.

To Betty Lewison,
my great mother-in-law
and owner of SO many shoes!
—W.C.L.

For Colleen and Nancy
—T.G.

Text copyright © 2000 by Wendy Cheyette Lewison.
Illustrations copyright © 2000 by Tony Griego.
All rights reserved. Published by Scholastic Inc.
SCHOLASTIC, HELLO READER, CARTWHEEL BOOKS and associated logos are trademarks and/or registered trademarks of Scholastic Inc.

Library of Congress Cataloging-in-Publication Data

Lewison, Wendy Cheyette.
    So many boots / by Wendy Cheyette Lewison; illustrated by Tony Griego.
        p. cm. — (My first hello reader!)
    "Cartwheel books."
    Summary: Looking forward to playing in the rain, Little Bug finds that by the time he has put on his eight pairs of boots, the rain has stopped. Includes related activities and game cards.
    ISBN 0-439-09865-3
    [1. Insects Fiction. 2. Rain and rainfall Fiction. 3. Boots Fiction 4. Stories in rhyme.]
        I. Griego, Tony, ill. II. Title. III. Series.
    PZ8.3.L5925o 2000   99-30153
    [E]—dc21   CIP

10 9 8 7 6 5 4 3 2 1   00 01 02 03 04

Printed in the U.S.A.   24

First printing, March 2000

SO MANY BOOTS

by Wendy Cheyette Lewison
Illustrated by Tony Griego

My First Hello Reader!
With Game Cards

SCHOLASTIC INC.

New York   Toronto   London   Auckland   Sydney
Mexico City   New Delhi   Hong Kong

What a rainy, rainy day!

Little Bug would love to play.

He puts on his raincoat.

He puts on his hat.

Bright red boots

come after that.

One boot, two boots,

three boots on.

Four boots, five boots,

six boots on.

On goes seven.

On goes eight.

So many boots. . . .

Now he's too late!

The rain has stopped.

Too bad, too bad.

Poor Little Bug

feels very sad.

Wait, Little Bug!

What was that?

Drip, drip, drip.

Splat, splat, splat.

Big, wet raindrops start to fall.

And who is ready, boots and all?

One Little Bug

who will get his wish!

Eight little boots go

splish, splish, splish!

Understanding the Story

Why was Little Bug sad?

Why was he too late to play in the rain?

Have you ever been late for something you wanted to do? What made you late? Were you disappointed? Why?

Hidden Pictures

Eight boots are hidden around Little Bug's house.
Can you help him find them?

B is for Bug

Bug starts with the letter B.
Circle the things that begin with the letter B.

Rhyme Time

It's time to rhyme! Words that rhyme sound alike.
Can you match each word to the picture
whose name rhymes with it?

play

rug

rain

fish

bug

tray

splish

train

How Many?

Which word tells how many things are in each row?

one   two

three   four

five   six

seven   eight

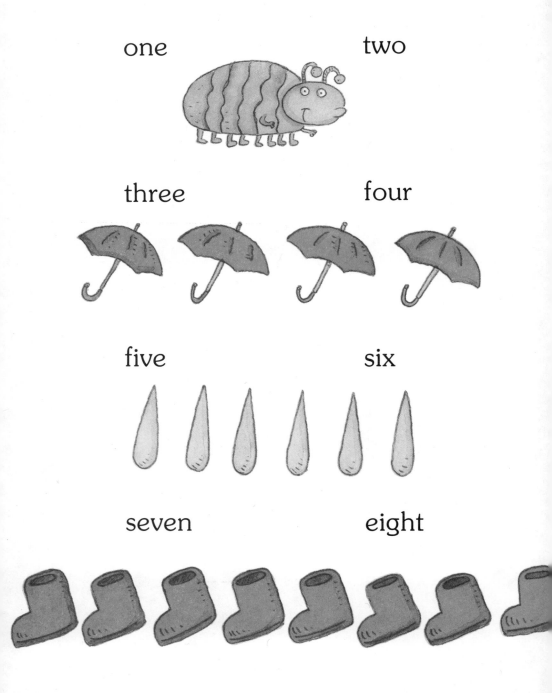

An A-MAZE-ing Bug!

Can you help Little Bug find his house?
Use your finger to show him the way.

ANSWERS

Understanding the Story

Little Bug was sad because he was too late to play in the rain.

Little Bug was too late because, by the time he put all his boots on all his feet, the rain had stopped.

Answers will vary to the last question.

Hidden Pictures

The eight hidden boots are circled here.

Rhyme Time

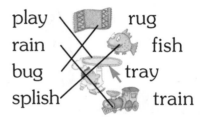

play   rug
rain   fish
bug   tray
splish   train

How Many?

one

four

six

eight

B is for Bug

These begin with the letter B.

An A-MAZE-ing Bug

The way through the maze is shown here.